www.FlowerpotPress.com
DJS-0912-0119
ISBN: 978-1-68461-260-4
Made in China/Fabriqué en Chine

The Ants Go Marching One By One

Frankie O'Connor

Illustrated by Nicole Groot

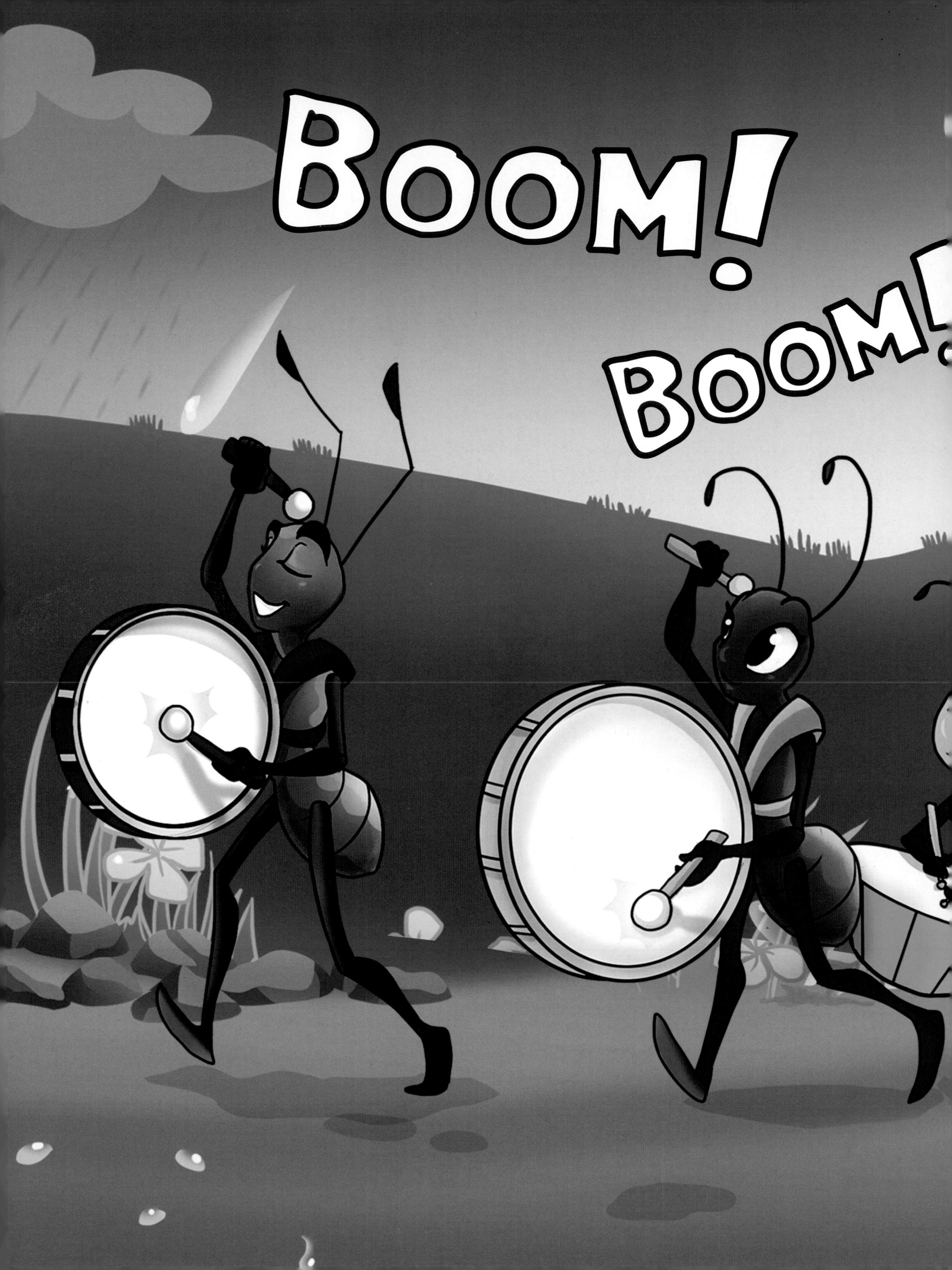
BOOM!
BOOM!

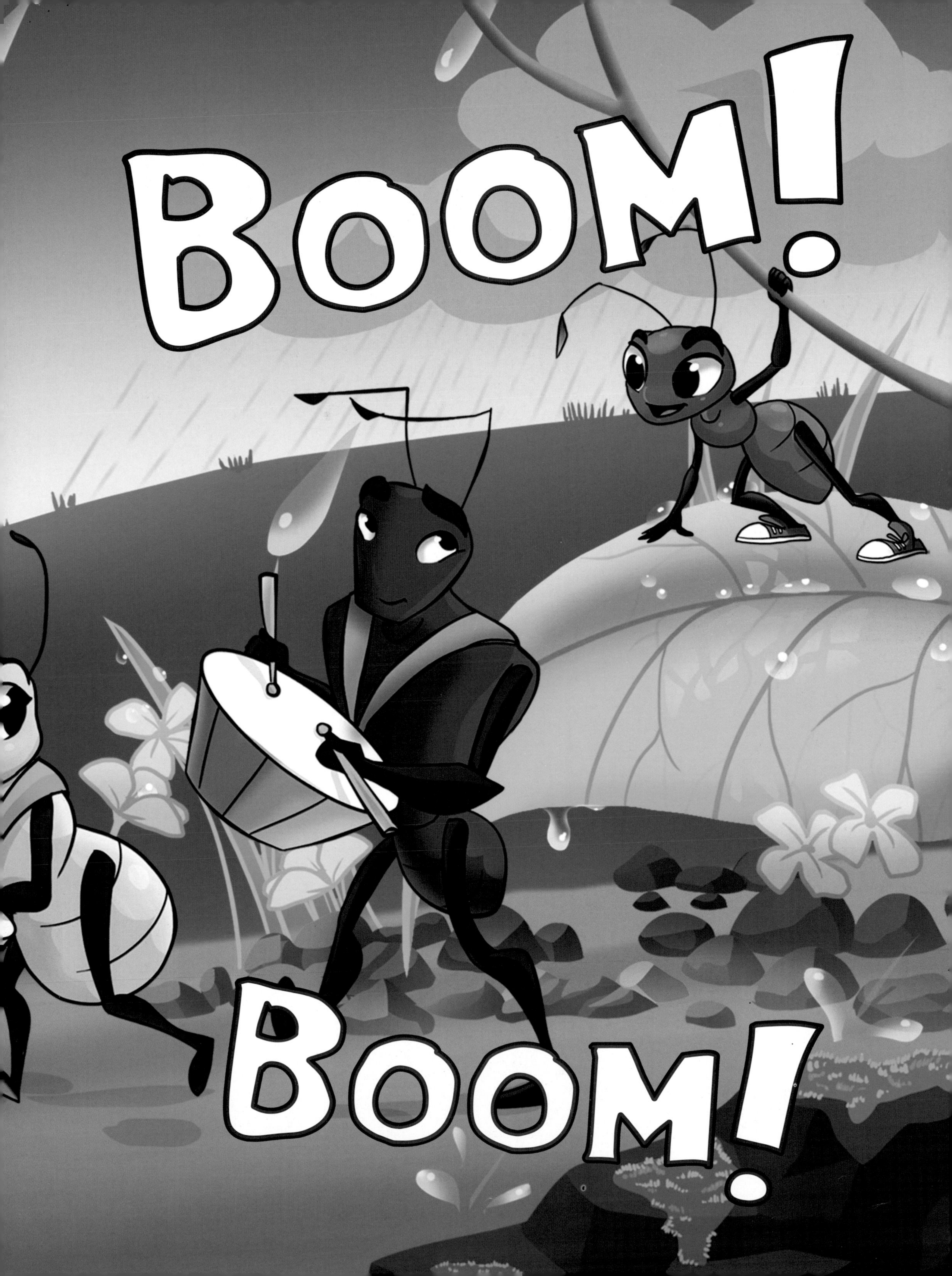
BOOM!
BOOM!

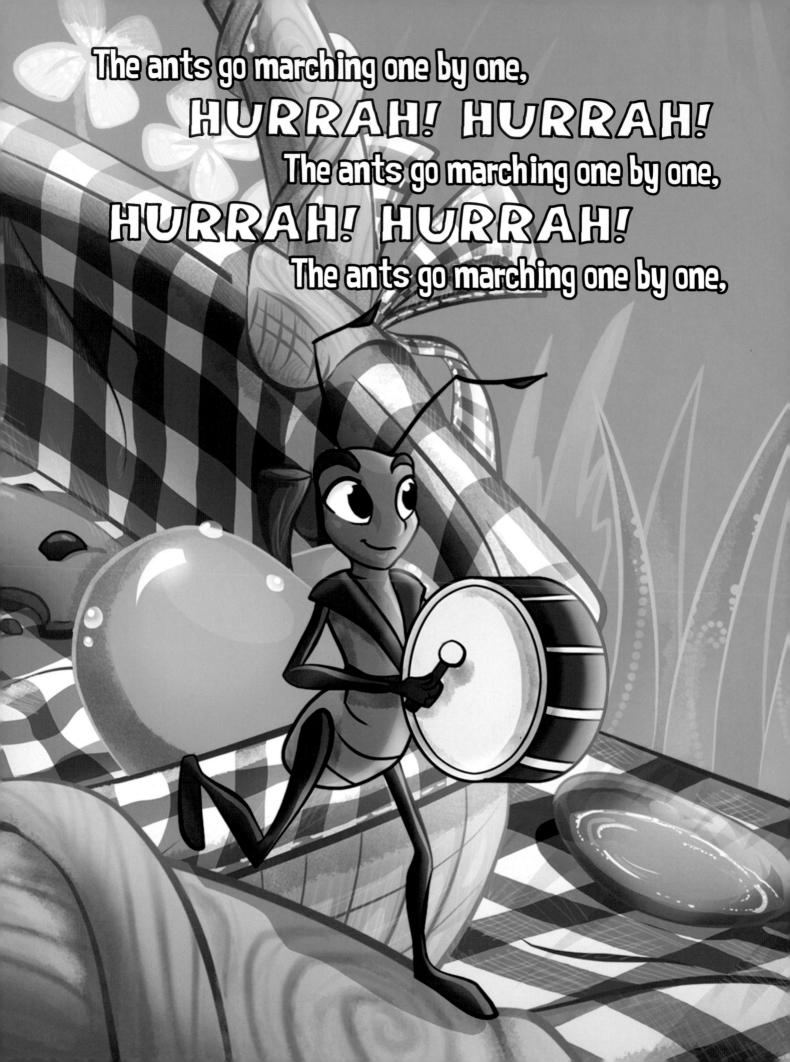

the little one stops to have some fun,
and they all go marching down,
to the ground,
to get out of the rain.

the little one stops to water ski,
and they all go marching down,
to the ground,
to get out of the rain.

BOOM!

BOOM!

BOOM!

The ants go marching four by four,
HURRAH! HURRAH!
The ants go marching four by four,
HURRAH! HURRAH!
The ants go marching four by four,

The ants go marching five by five,

HURRAH! HURRAH!

The ants go marching five by five,

HURRAH! HURRAH!

The ants go marching five by five,

the little one stops to clean home plate,
and they all go marching down,
to the ground,
to get out of the rain.

BOOM!
BOOM!
BOOM!

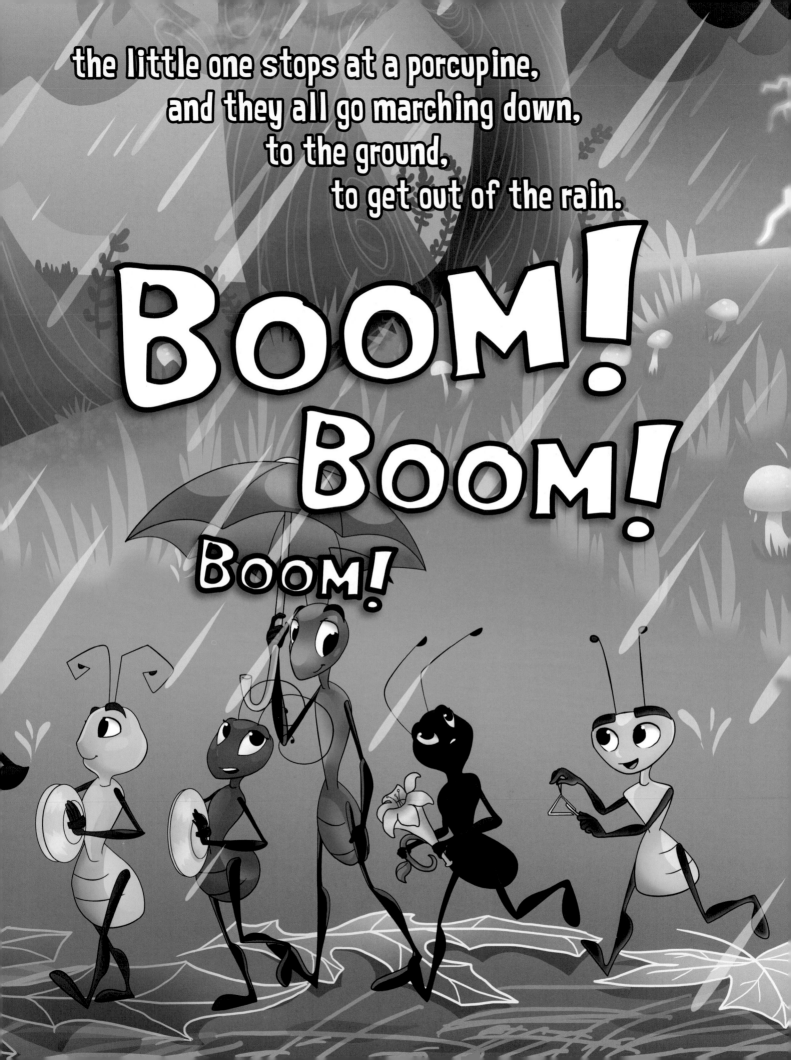

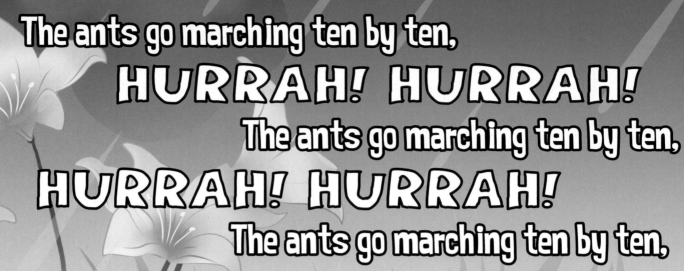

The ants go marching ten by ten,
HURRAH! HURRAH!
The ants go marching ten by ten,
HURRAH! HURRAH!
The ants go marching ten by ten,

and they all go marching down,
to the ground,
to get out of the rain.

BOOM!
BOOM!
BOOM!
BOOM!

BOOM!

BOOM!

BOOM!